W9-CFG-838

This book belongs to this Marshalltown Young Person

NAME: Stella

DATE: 4-26-2021

Marshall T. Trowel and Family

CONCRETE

WORK HARD. WORK TOGETHER.

A Marshalltown Book for Young People who Love Construction

Written by Joe Carter

Illustrated by Hanna Carter

Marshalltown Company, 104 South 8th Avenue, Marshalltown, Iowa 50158
641-753-5999 | 800-888-0127 | www.marshalltown.com

Printed in the United States of America by Christian Printers, Inc.

ISBN: 978-0-578-41854-4

FOR THE YOUNG PERSON who is reading this book with their parent, grandparent, older brother or sister, or other special adult in their life, I wish them all the same moments that were created when my wife and I enjoyed books with our children.

I started writing this book in 2002 when my three children were 6, 8 and 12. My wife Janelle and I read books to them every night. It was a time all of us treasured. I wanted to take those treasured moments and turn them into a book that would take my world in the construction industry and pair it with those cute characters who bring to life many of the tools of the job. Some of those characters hold the names of my three children — Mike, Hanna and Sam.

Janelle and I are so proud of all three of our children. Each one is out of school and embarking on a career that they've chosen, and a career that seems fitting for each of them based upon the interests they had as a young child. There were many times for teachings during their childhood and I'm confident that they work hard and they work together with their peers to bring about great results — the message of this book.

I dedicate this book to my beautiful children, my beautiful wife and to the rest of my wonderful family who have encouraged me throughout my life. I am blessed to have them close in my heart.

I hope that you will also hold close in your heart, the young person who is reading this book with you. Maybe this young person will fall in love with construction and embark on a career that helps build the world with wonderful things. But no matter what, I hope this young person decides to work hard at whatever useful career they choose.

It has been a special joy for me to share this book-writing experience with my daughter Hanna. She used her artistic talents to bring to life each of the characters I had envisioned. It was a pleasure to work with her to create this book. I couldn't have done it without her. I don't know how a father could be more proud.

-Joe Carter

MASON CONSTRUCTION
MARSHALLTOWN, IOWA

Mr. Mason had another important day planned. It was early April in Marshalltown, Iowa and the weather was finally turning warm. Customers were starting to line up with new jobs for pouring concrete.

Mr. Mason would make a beautiful concrete driveway for Miss Bella Bright the next morning. He wanted to be well rested to do the best job he could. Mr. Mason went to bed and quickly drifted off to sleep dreaming about how wonderful the new driveway would look when he finished!

Meanwhile, in the tool trailer, there was quite a conversation going on among all the concrete tools. Marshall T. Trowel tried to prepare everyone for the big workday ahead.

" We need to lay our heads down and get some sleep. Each of you should know that Mr. Mason will want us to be well-rested for tomorrow!"

However, Tabby Tie-Wire Twister was all excited after her big day at Bella's home. Mr. Mason started early that morning, setting the forms square, solid and at just the right slope. Those forms would hold the concrete when it was poured the next day.

Then Pat Plate Compactor moved around every square inch of the gravel base inside the forms to properly compact the area.

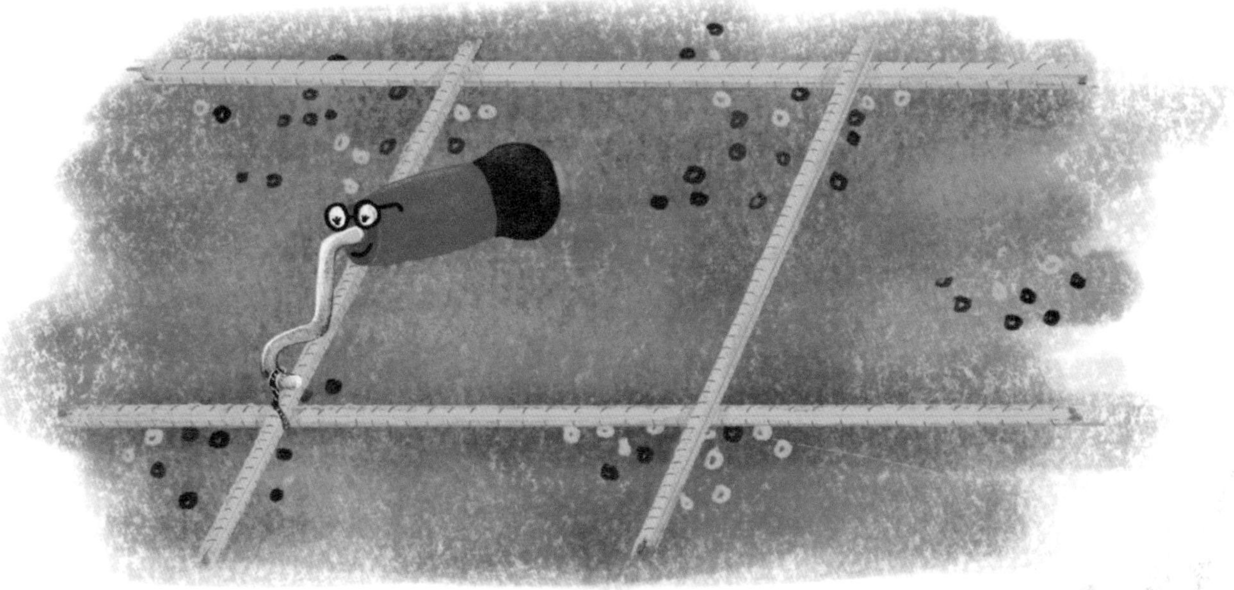

Finally, Tabby neatly tied all the rebar together, which would help to reinforce the concrete. When Mr. Mason left Bella's home, the site was ready for the morning concrete pour.

Tabby had done her work and had no interest in going to sleep. She yelled out to all the tools,

"WHO WANTS TO

STAY UP AND HAVE SOME FUN

Peggy Placer was quick to respond.

"I've got to be ready to work first thing tomorrow morning. Mr. Mason is counting on me. No one is more important than me because as soon as that concrete truck shows up and starts pouring concrete, Mr. Mason will need me to put the concrete exactly where he wants it. The rest of you will just be sitting around waiting for me to do my work."

Sammy Screed was hurt by Peggy Placer's words.

"Mr. Mason told me that I was the most important tool of all because I keep everything level and smooth."

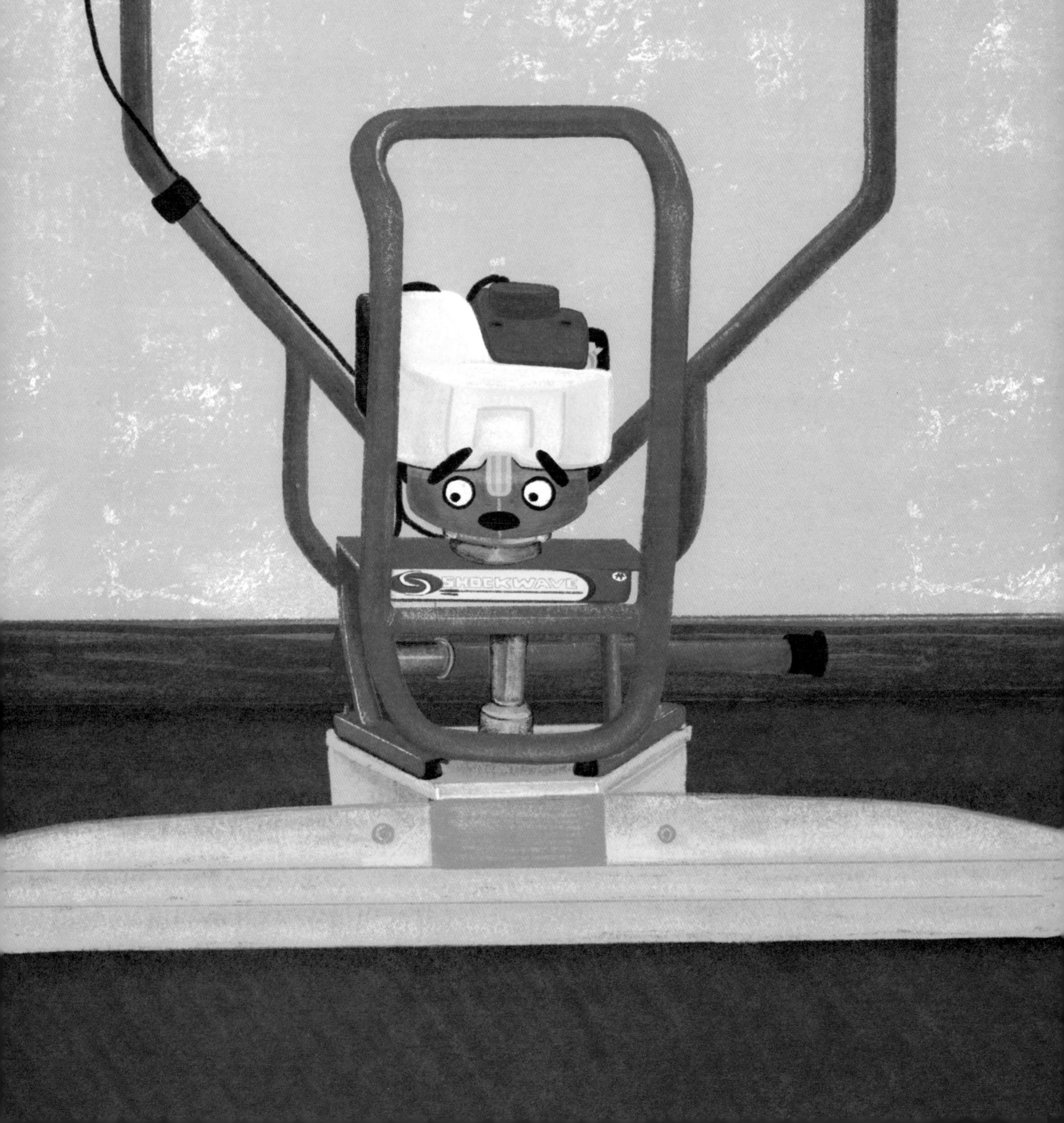

Marshall T. Trowel calmly said,

" All of you know that you are important to Mr. Mason and that each of you needs to do your job to be able to get the entire project done well. Tabby, you did your work today, and I'm sure that Mr. Mason is proud of you, but the rest of us have to be ready for our jobs tomorrow. Let's all get some sleep and be rested for the important work we need to do in the morning."

Tabby Tie-Wire Twister knew Marshall T. Trowel was right. She spoke more softly, saying,

"We'll be quiet and just relax after our hard day at work. That way, the rest of you will be able to sleep soundly. Good night Marshall."

All the MARSHALLTOWN tools agreed, so they laid their heads down and dozed off to sleep.

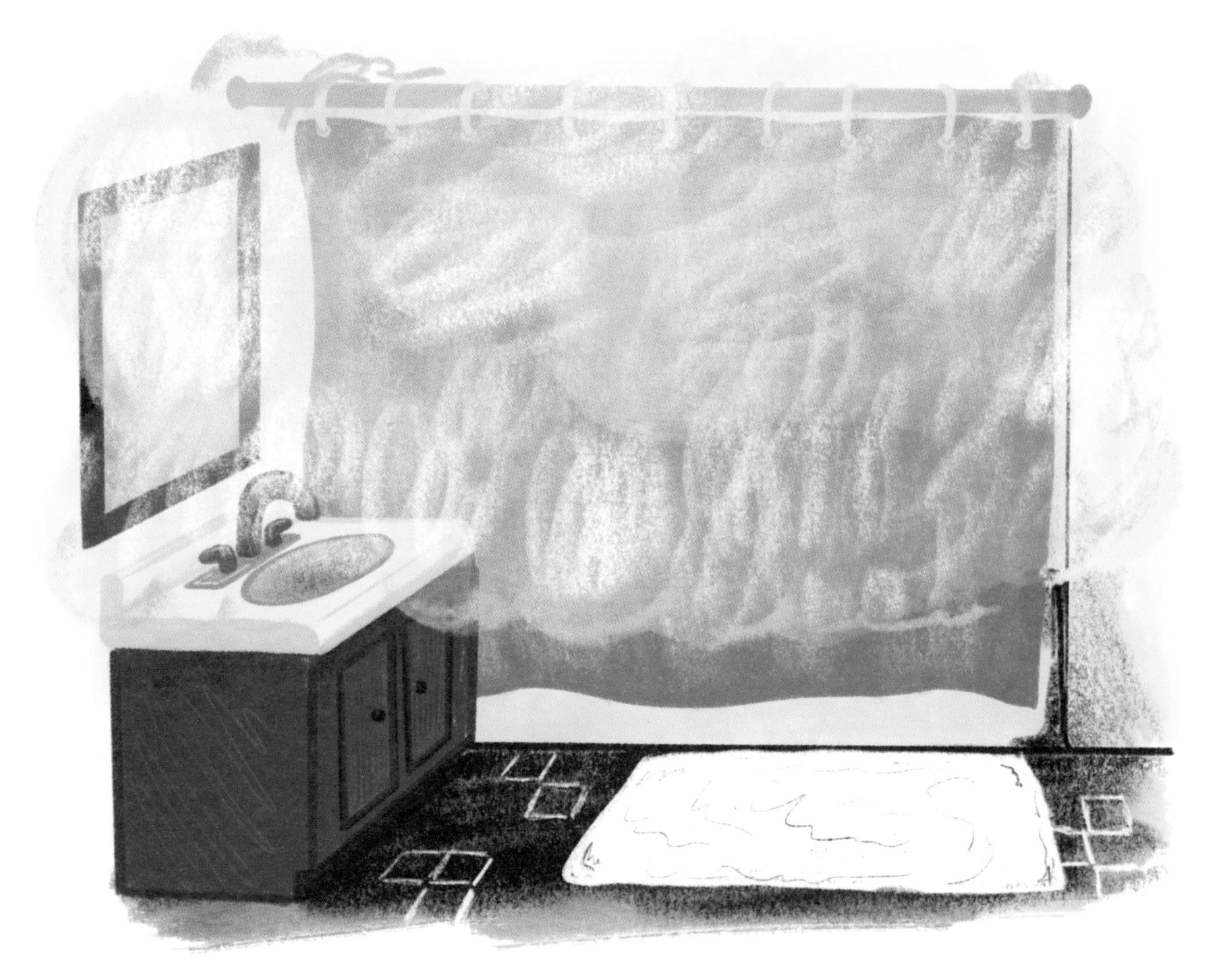

Mr. Mason awoke bright and early the next morning. After he brushed his teeth, showered, and ate a healthy breakfast, Mr. Mason hopped into his pick-up truck and drove away with his tool trailer following close behind, all headed to Bella's home.

As Mr. Mason drove to
Miss Bella Bright's home,
the sun rose above the horizon
on this beautiful, warm morning.

He put his window down to enjoy the nice
spring air. As Mr. Mason drove he could
hear the birds chirping and he could see
the trees beginning to bloom. Mr. Mason
was all set for a wonderful day!

1234

Once Mr. Mason arrived at Bella's home, he checked the forms and made certain everything was ready for the concrete. The site looked perfect!

Mr. Mason walked back to his trailer
and unloaded Peggy Placer and
Sammy Screed. He knew that he'd need
their help shortly after the concrete truck
arrived. Mr. Mason also placed
Mike Margin Trowel in his back pocket.
Mike was a trusted partner in every
one of Mr. Mason's concrete pours.

Mike sat proudly on Mr. Mason's hip
waiting for the time when his work
would be needed. Hanna Hand Float
waited in the grass. She would be needed
at a moment's notice, so Hanna waited
with a quiet pride too.

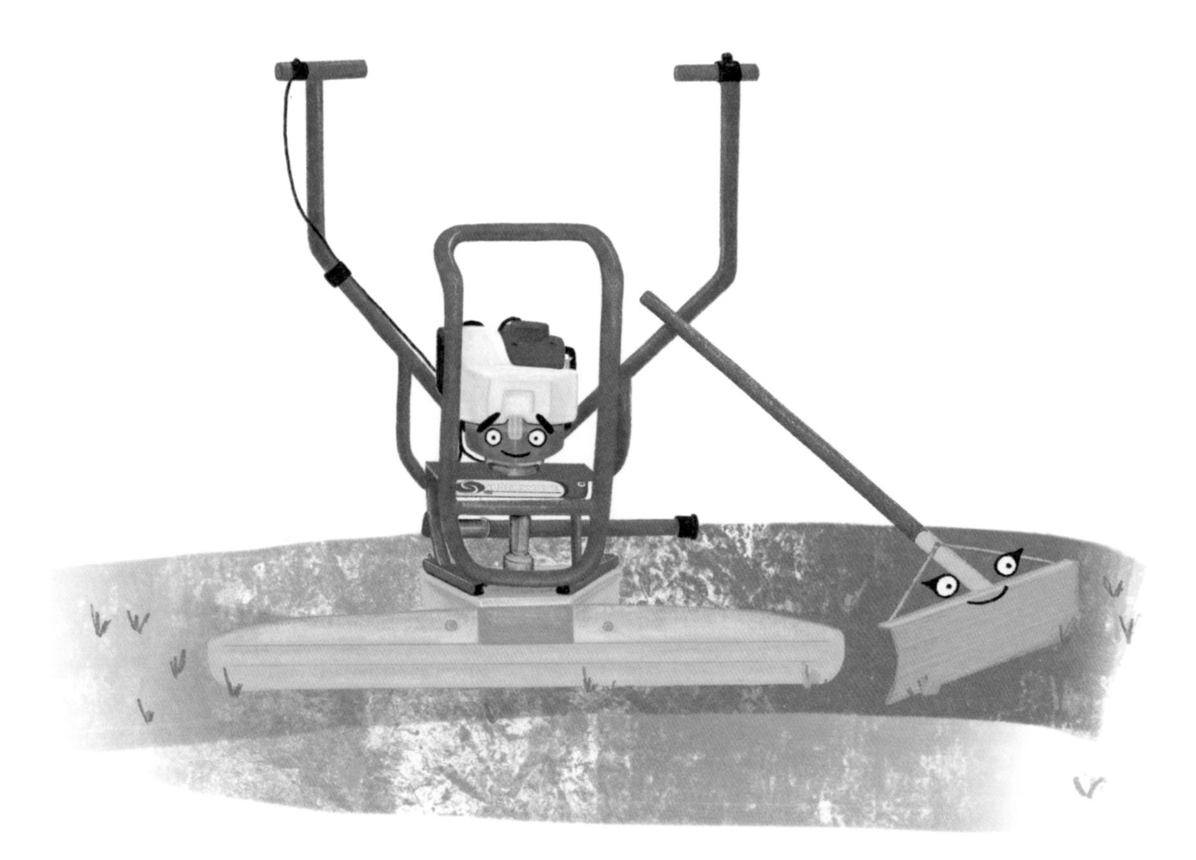

The concrete truck arrived at Bella's home. Daisy the Driver jumped from her truck and met Mr. Mason to discuss the pour. She prepared the chutes and then began sending the concrete down into the forms.

Peggy Placer was quick to move the concrete into the corners, all the way to the edges of the forms and all the time trying to keep a consistent height of concrete across the driveway. Peggy perspired from all the work.

Sammy Screed revved his engine and stepped into action right behind Peggy Placer. He moved across the driveway to smooth the concrete.

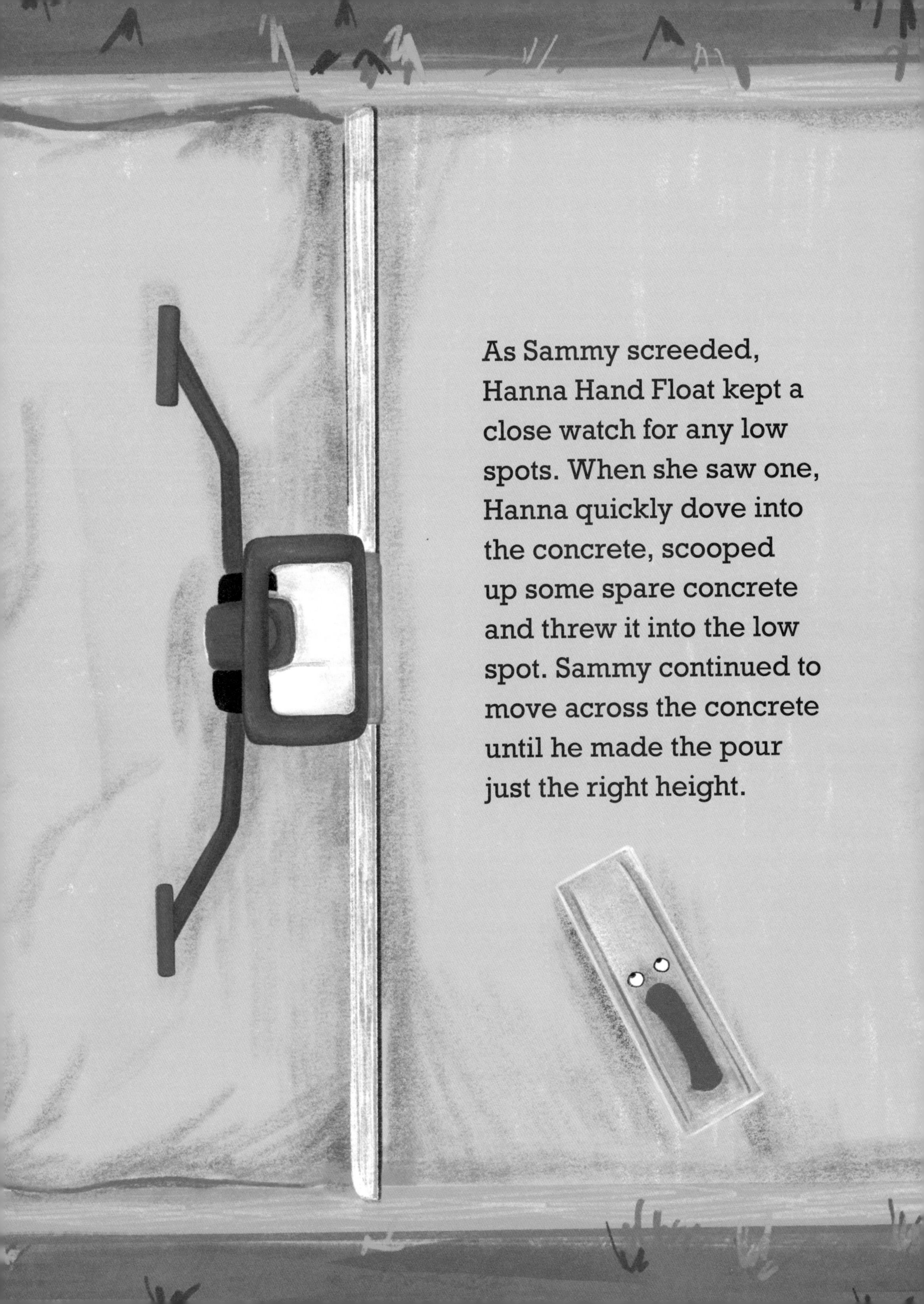

As Sammy screeded, Hanna Hand Float kept a close watch for any low spots. When she saw one, Hanna quickly dove into the concrete, scooped up some spare concrete and threw it into the low spot. Sammy continued to move across the concrete until he made the pour just the right height.

Once all the concrete had
been placed and screeded,
Daisy cleaned her chutes
and drove her truck away.
Mr. Mason knew that his
own work had just begun.

Then Billy Bull Float went to work. He carried Rocky Rock-it on board to make the tipping of Billy's blade so easy. Oscar Octagon Pole turned Rocky in just the right direction to make the ride nice and smooth.

Once Billy Bull Float
had smoothed the entire
surface, Edgar Edger
slid around the
outside edges of the
concrete, just inside
the forms, to make
a rounded edge.

Mike Margin Trowel made his way, sliding
down along the forms to help separate the
edge of the concrete from the forms. With
Edgar and Mike doing their good work,
the forms would later be pulled away
from the concrete without trouble.

Then Grover Groover
made his way, cutting through
the concrete, from one side to the
other. His big bit created a straight
control joint so that Bella wouldn't
have to worry about cracks ever
appearing in her driveway.

Finally, it was time for Marshall T. Trowel to finish the job. Marshall waved over the top surface of the concrete making things smoother and smoother as he worked. He pressed his blade against the surface of the concrete, moving across the entire slab until the job was done.

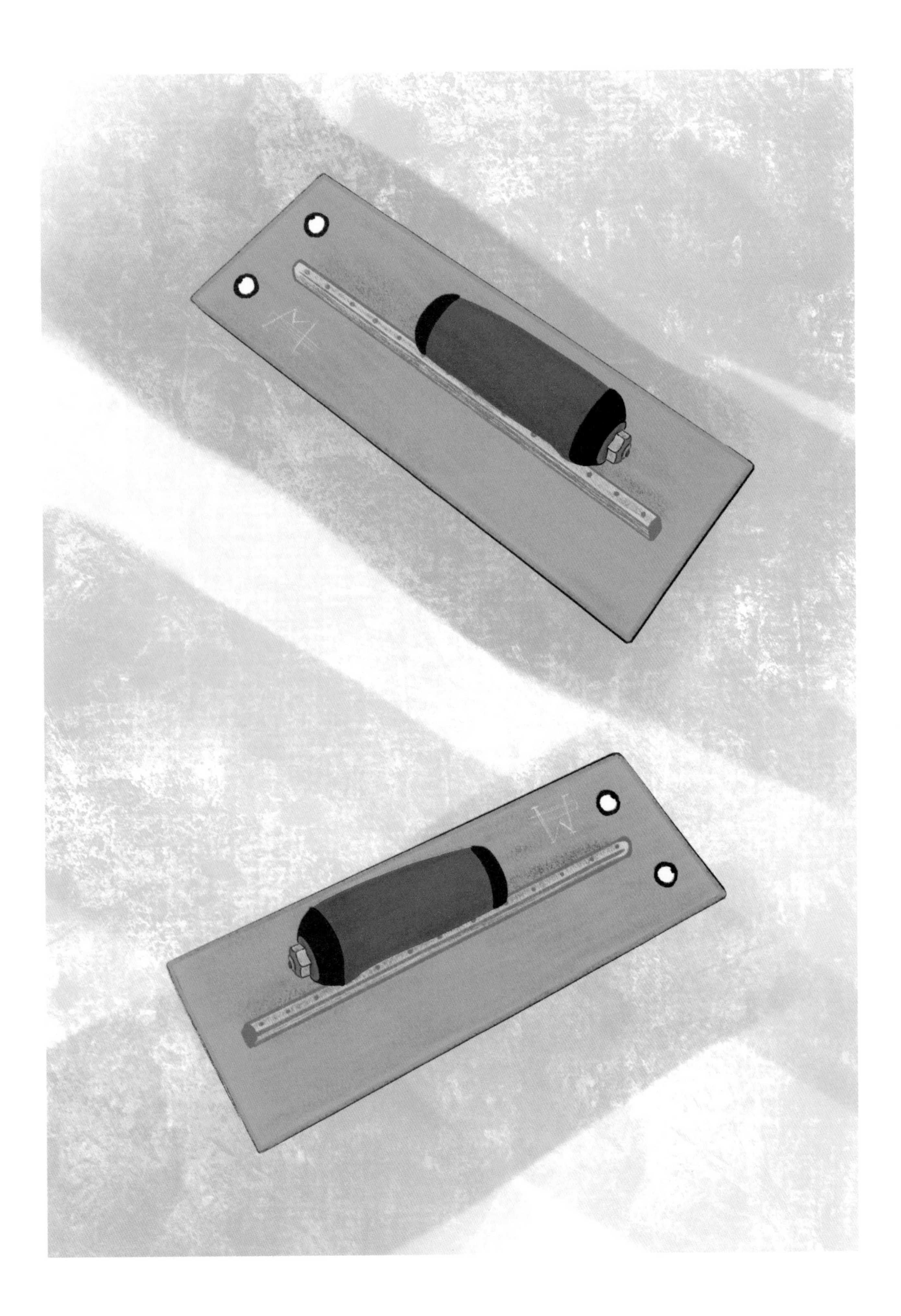

As Marshall T. Trowel finished his work, he smiled at all the tools and said,

"Each and every one of you did a great job. You worked so hard and so well. If one of you had been missing, we would not have done such a good job for Miss Bella Bright. I'm so proud of all of you."

Mr. Mason helped get all the tools back into his trailer for the ride home. Bella was so pleased with her new concrete driveway and she smiled and waved goodbye to her new friends.

JOE CARTER is the husband to his wonderful wife Janelle and the father to three fantastic children — Michael, Hanna and Samuel. Joe grew up in Hanlontown, a small, northern Iowa community, graduated from North Central-Manly High School and later, from Iowa State University with an Industrial Engineering degree. Joe worked as an engineer for General Motors and Rockwell International before he began a long career with MARSHALLTOWN, a U.S. manufacturer of high-quality construction tools.

Between times of working as an engineer, Joe graduated from law school at the University of Arkansas and practiced law with Strong and Associates in Springfield, Missouri. He returned to MARSHALLTOWN and moved to Marshalltown, Iowa. In 1998 Joe became the president of MARSHALLTOWN and later added CEO to that title.

Joe met the love of his life, Janelle Andersen at Iowa State University where they both graduated in Industrial Engineering. Janelle and Joe later married and were fortunate enough to raise their three fabulous children.

HANNA CARTER is an illustrator and graphic designer. She grew up in Marshalltown, Iowa and graduated from Iowa State University in Ames, Iowa. She moved to Oregon after college in 2016.

Hanna has loved both books and drawing for as long as she can remember. In fact, her first job was at the Marshalltown Public Library, where she spent a lot of her time leafing through childrens books. She's pretty psyched that she got to make her own childrens book with her dad.

Hanna lives in Portland, Oregon with her boyfriend and many, many books.

www.marshalltown.com